Der Fuchs und der Kranich
- eine Äsopische Fabel

The Fox and the Crane
- an Aesop's Fable

retold by Dawn Casey

illustrated by Jago

German translation by Friederike Barkow

Fox started it. He invited Crane to dinner....
When Crane arrived at Fox's house he saw dishes
of every colour and kind lined the shelves.
Big ones, tall ones, short ones, small ones.
The table was set with two dishes. Two flat shallow dishes.

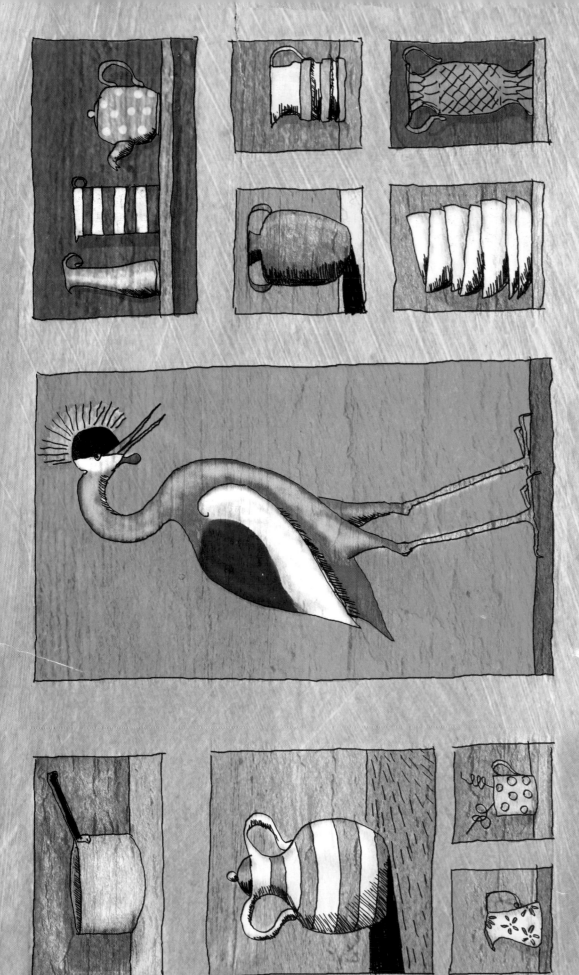

Der Fuchs machte den Anfang. Er lud den Kranich zum Essen ein...
Als der Kranich bei dem Haus, in dem der Fuchs wohnte, ankam, sah
er Geschirr in allen Farben und Größen in den Fächern stehen. Große,
hohe, niedrige, kleine Gefäße.
Der Tisch war mit zwei Stücken gedeckt. Zwei flachen Tellern.

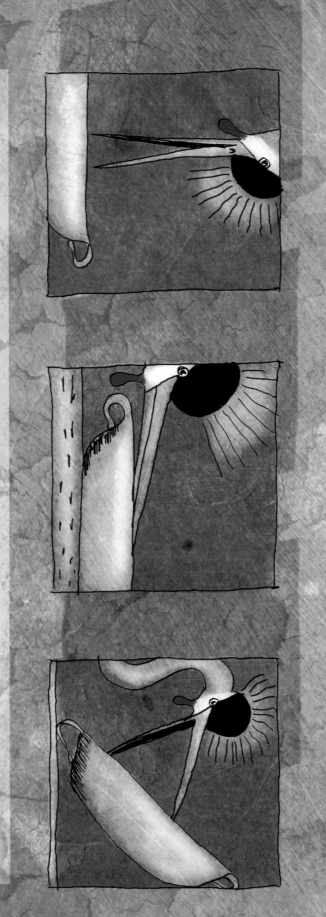

Der Kranich pickte und hackte mit seinem schmalen, langen Schnabel auf dem Teller herum. Aber so sehr er sich auch bemühte, er konnte nicht einmal einen Tropfen der Suppe in den Schnabel bekommen.

Crane pecked and he picked with his long thin beak. But no matter how hard he tried he could not get even a sip of the soup.

Der Fuchs beobachtete wie der Kranich sich plagte und kicherte. Er hob seine eigene Suppe zu seinen Lippen und SCHLIPP, SCHLAPP, SCHLÜRF schleckte er seinen Teller leer.

„Aah, delikat!", spottete er und wischte sich die Schnurrhaare mit dem Rücken seiner Pfote.

„Oh Kranich, du hast ja deine Suppe gar nicht angerührt", sagte der Fuchs grinsend. „ES TUT MIR SO LEID, daß sie dir nicht geschmeckt hat", fügte er hinzu und bemühte sich, nicht in schallendes Gelächter auszubrechen.

Fox watched Crane struggling and sniggered. He lifted his own soup to his lips, and with a SIP, SLOP, SLURP he lapped it all up.

"Ahhhh, delicious!" he scoffed, wiping his whiskers with the back of his paw.

"Oh Crane, you haven't touched your soup," said Fox with a smirk. "I AM sorry you didn't like it," he added, trying not to snort with laughter.

Der Kranich hielt seinen Schnabel. Er besah sich das Mahl. Er besah den Teller. Er sah den Fuchs an und lächelte.

„Lieber Fuchs, habe vielen Dank für deine freundliche Einladung", sagte der Kranich höflich. „Bitte erlaube mir, sie zu erwidern und komm zum Essen zu mir."

Als der Fuchs beim Kranich ankam, war das Fenster offen. Ein köstlicher Duft strömte heraus. Der Fuchs hob seine Schnauze und schnupperte. Das Wasser lief ihm im Mund zusammen. Sein Magen begann zu knurren. Er leckte sich die Lippen.

Crane said nothing. He looked at the meal. He looked at the dish. He looked at Fox, and smiled. "Dear Fox, thank you for your kindness," said Crane politely. "Please let me repay you – come to dinner at my house."

When Fox arrived the window was open. A delicious smell drifted out. Fox lifted his snout and sniffed. His mouth watered. His stomach rumbled. He licked his lips.

„Mein lieber Fuchs, komm herein", sagte der Kranich und breitete freundlich seine Flügel aus. Der Fuchs drängte sich ungeduldig an ihm vorbei. Er sah Geschirr in allen Farben und Formen in den Fächern stehen. Rote, blaue, alte Stücke, neue Stücke. Der Tisch war aber nur mit zwei Stücken gedeckt; zwei schmalen, hohen Gefäßen.

"My dear Fox, do come in," said Crane, extending his wing graciously. Fox pushed past. He saw dishes of every colour and kind lined the shelves. Red ones, blue ones, old ones, new ones. The table was set with two dishes. Two tall narrow dishes.

Der Fuchs leckte und schlürfte, aber mit seiner kurzen, kleinen Schnauze konnte er keinen Bissen erreichen, so sehr er sich auch bemühte.

Fox licked and he lapped with his short little snout.
But no matter how hard he tried he could not
get even a mouthful of the meal.

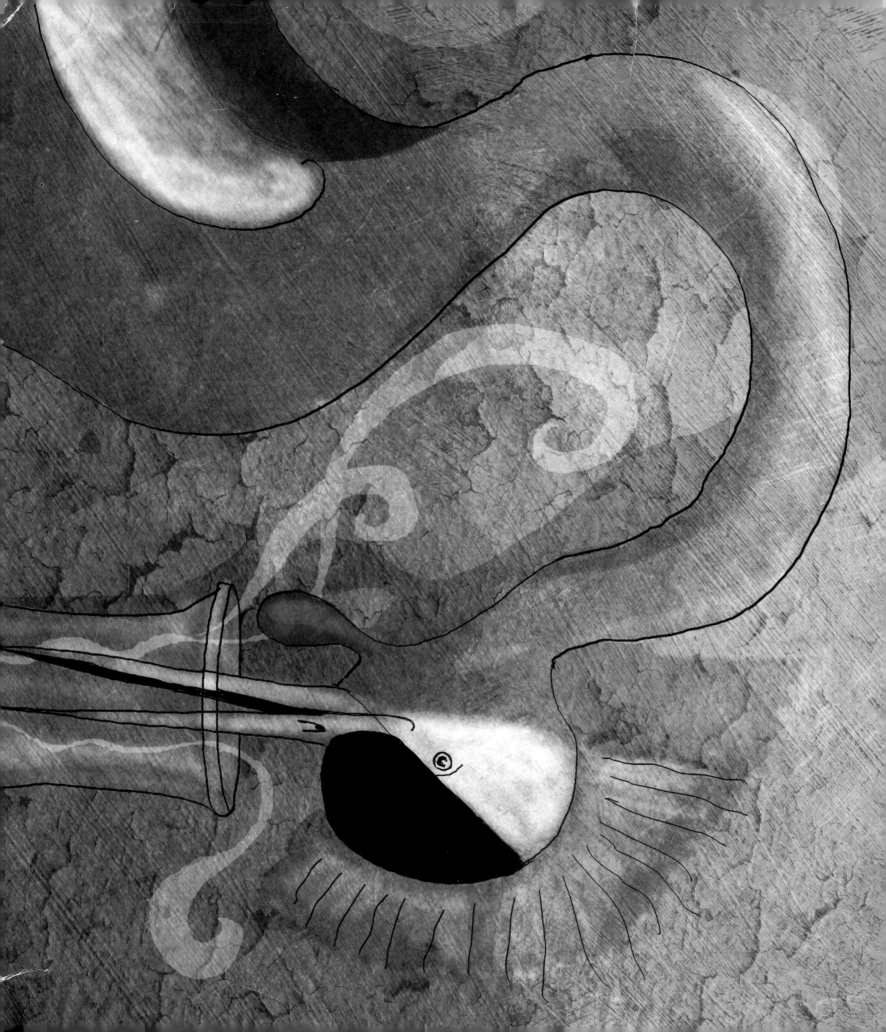

Der Kranich aß langsam und genoss jeden Bissen.
„Lieber Fuchs, hab vielen Dank, daß du zum Essen gekommen bist",
sagte der Kranich lächelnd, „es war mir ein Vergnügen, dir deine Güte
zu vergelten".

Dem Fuchs knurrte und gurgelte der Magen.
Und als er nach Hause ging, war er noch immer so hungrig wie zuvor.

Crane ate his meal very slowly, savouring every mouthful.
"Dear Fox, thank you so much for coming," he smiled,
"it has been a pleasure to repay your kindness."

Fox's tummy gurgled and grumbled.
And when he went home, he was still hungry.

The Fox and the Crane

Writing Activity:
Read the story. Explain that we can write our own fable by changing the characters.

Discuss the different animals you could use, bearing in mind what different kinds of dishes they would need! For example, instead of the fox and the crane you could have a tiny mouse and a tall giraffe.

Write an example together as a class, then give the children the opportunity to write their own. Children who need support could be provided with a writing frame.

Art Activity:
Provide a variety of vessels: bowls, jugs, vases, mugs… Children can use these to investigate capacity:

Compare the containers and order them from smallest to largest.

Estimate the capacity of each container.

Young children can use non-standard measures e.g. 'about 3 beakers full'.

Check estimates by filling the container with coloured liquid ('soup') or dry lentils.

Older children can use standard measures such as a litre jug, and measure using litres and millilitres. How near were the estimates?

Label each vessel with its capacity.

Maths Activity:
Dishes of every colour and kind! Create them from clay, salt dough, play dough… Make them, paint them, decorate them…

The King of the Forest

Writing Activity:
Children can write their own fables by changing the setting of this story. Think about what kinds of animals you would find in a different setting. For example how about 'The King of the Arctic' starring an arctic fox and a polar bear!

Storytelling Activity:
Draw a long path down a roll of paper showing the route Fox took through the forest. The children can add their own details, drawing in the various scenes and re-telling the story orally with model animals.

If you are feeling ambitious you could chalk the path onto the playground so that children can act out the story using appropriate noises and movements! (They could even make masks to wear, decorated with feathers, woollen fur, sequin scales etc.)

Music Activity:
Children choose a forest animal. Then select an instrument that will make a sound that matches the way their animal looks and moves. Encourage children to think about musical features such as volume, pitch and rhythm. For example a loud, low, plodding rhythm played on a drum could represent an elephant.

Children perform their animal sounds. Can the class guess the animal?

Children can play their pieces in groups, to create a forest soundscape.

Der König des Waldes

- eine Chinesische Fabel

The King of the Forest

- a Chinese Fable

retold by Dawn Casey

illustrated by Jago

German translation
by Friederike Barkow

Der Fuchs ging durch den Wald, als er hörte wie sich
etwas in dem hohen Gras bewegte.

RASCHEL Etwas großes.

BLINK Etwas mit gelben Augen.

BLITZ Etwas mit Zähnen wie Messer.

Fox was walking in the forest when he heard something moving
in the long grass.

RUSTLE Something big.

BLINK Something with yellow eyes.

FLASH Something with teeth like knives.

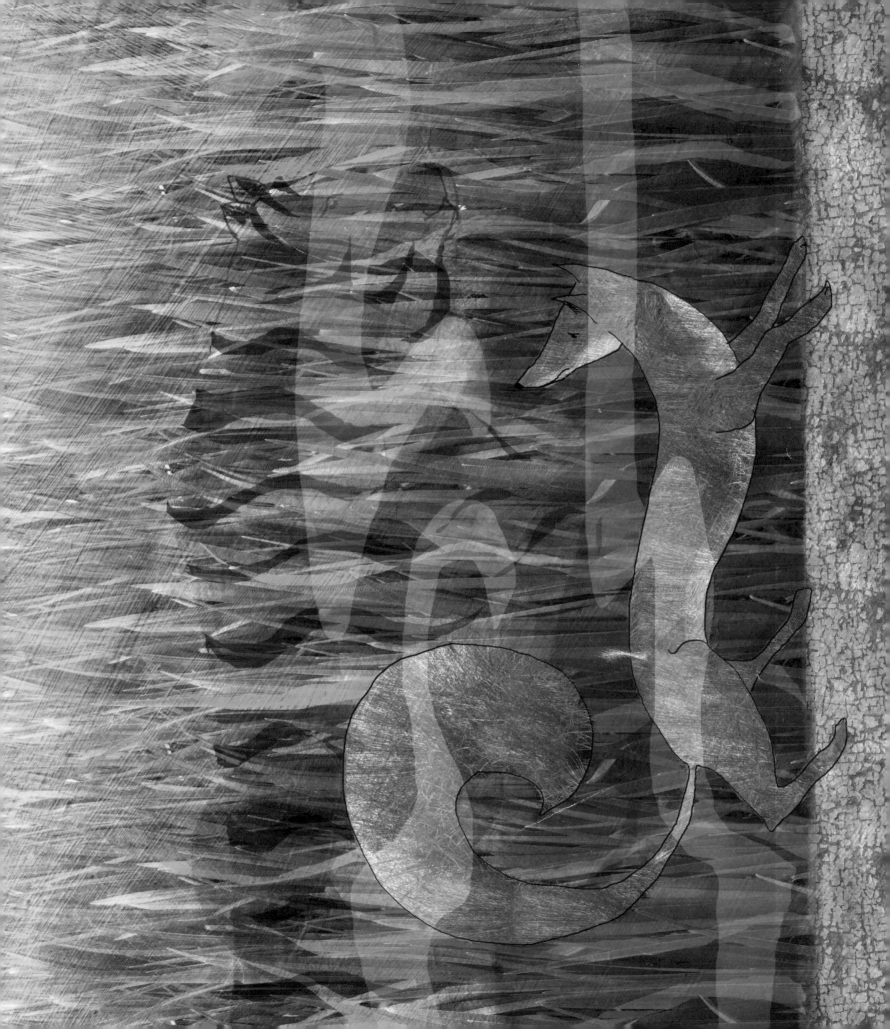

„Guten Morgen, kleiner Fuchs", sagte der Tiger und grinste, und sein Maul schien nur aus Zähnen zu bestehen.

Der Fuchs schluckte.

„Ich bin so froh dich zu treffen", schnurrte der Tiger, „ich fing gerade an, mich hungrig zu fühlen."

Der Fuchs dachte blitzschnell nach. „Was fällt dir ein!", sagte er. „Weißt du nicht, daß ich der König des Waldes bin?"

„Du! Der König des Waldes?", sagte der Tiger und schüttelte sich vor Lachen.

„Wenn du mir nicht glauben willst", sagte der Fuchs würdevoll, „dann folge mir und du wirst sehen, daß alle vor mir Angst haben."

„Das möcht ich erst mal sehen", sagte der Tiger.

Dann schlenderte der Fuchs durch den Wald. Der Tiger folgte ihm mit stolz erhobenem Schwanz bis...

"Good morning little fox," Tiger grinned, and his mouth was nothing but teeth.

Fox gulped.

"I am pleased to meet you," Tiger purred. "I was just beginning to feel hungry."

Fox thought fast. "How dare you!" he said. "Don't you know I'm the King of the Forest?"

"You! King of the Forest?" said Tiger, and he roared with laughter.

"If you don't believe me," replied Fox with dignity, "walk behind me and you'll see — everyone is scared of me."

"This I've got to see," said Tiger.

So Fox strolled through the forest. Tiger followed behind proudly, with his tail held high, until...

AARK!

Ein großer Falke mit einem hakenförmig gebognen Schnabel tauchte vor ihnen auf! Aber nach einem Blick auf den Tiger verschwand er flügelschlagend zwischen den Bäumen.

„Siehst du?", sagte der Fuchs. „Jeder hat Angst vor mir!"

„Unglaublich!", sagte der Tiger.

Der Fuchs schlenderte weiter durch den Wald. Der Tiger folgte ihm gelassen, aber sein Schwanz sank ein bisschen, bis...

SQUAWK!

A huge hook-beaked hawk! But the hawk took one look at Tiger and flapped into the trees.

"See?" said Fox. "Everyone is scared of me!"

"Unbelievable!" said Tiger.

Fox strode on through the forest.

Tiger followed behind lightly, with his tail drooping slightly, until...

BRUMMM!

Ein großer, schwarzer Bär! Aber der Bär warf einen Blick auf den Tiger und verschwand krachend in den Büschen. „Siehst du?", sagte der Fuchs. „Jeder hat Angst vor mir!" „Unbeschreiblich!", sagte der Tiger. Der Fuchs marschierte weiter durch den Wald. Der Tiger folgte ihm kleinlaut, sein Schwanz schleifte auf dem Boden, bis...

GROWL!

A big black bear! But the bear took one look at Tiger and crashed into the bushes. "See?" said Fox. "Everyone is scared of me!" "Incredible!" said Tiger.
Fox marched on through the forest. Tiger followed behind meekly, with his tail dragging on the forest floor, until...

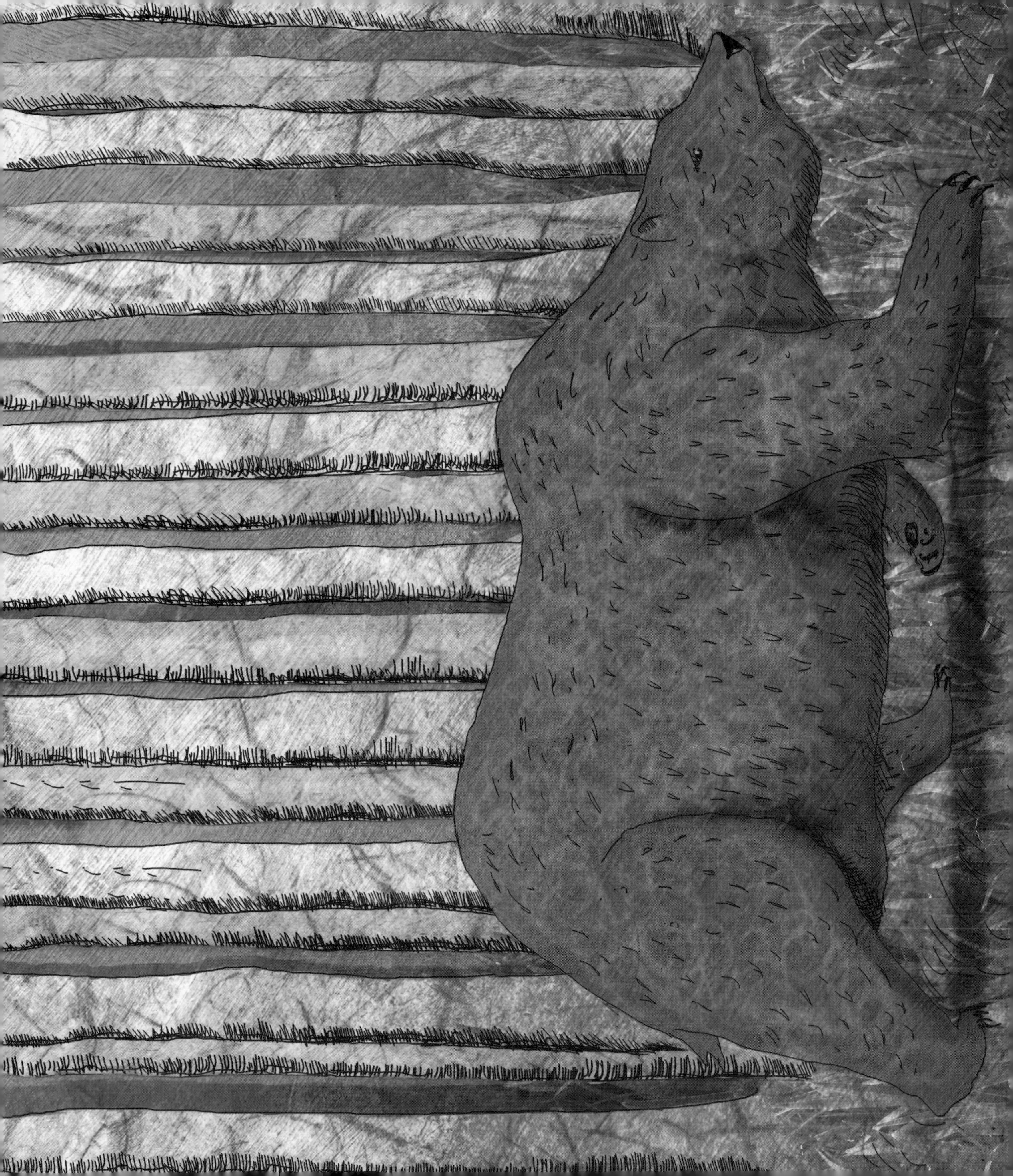

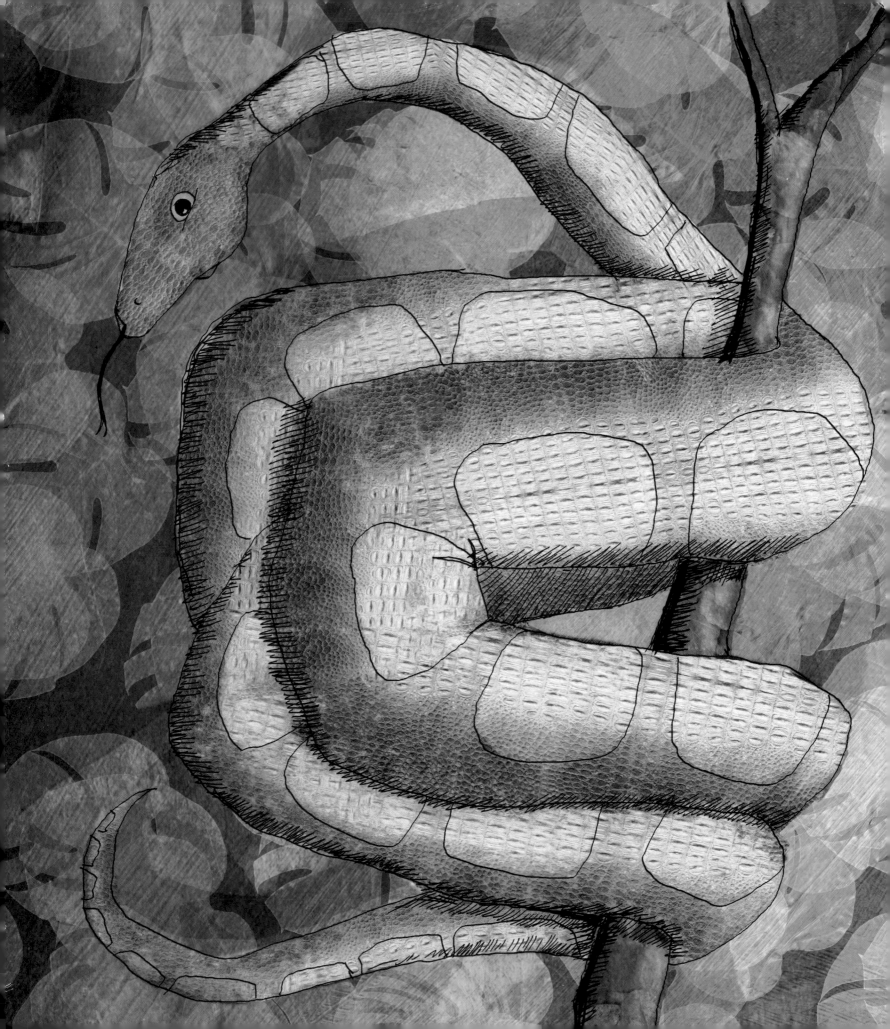

HISSS!
Eine geschmeidig gleitende Schlange! Aber die Schlange warf einen Blick auf den Tiger und glitt ins Unterholz. „SIEHST DU?", sagte der Fuchs. „JEDER HAT ANGST VOR MIR!"

HISSSSS!
A slinky slidey snake! But the snake took one look at Tiger and slithered into the undergrowth. "SEE?" said Fox. "EVERYONE IS SCARED OF ME!"

„Ich sehe es wohl", sagte der Tiger. „Du bist der König des Waldes und ich bin dein untertäniger Diener."

„Gut", sagte der Fuchs. „Dann mach dich davon!"

Und der Tiger ging mit seinem Schwanz zwischen den Beinen davon.

"I do see," said Tiger, "you are the King of the Forest and I am your humble servant."

"Good," said Fox. "Then, be gone!"

And Tiger went, with his tail between his legs.

„König des Waldes", sagte der Fuchs zu sich selbst und lächelte. Sein Lächeln wurde zu einem Grinsen und sein Grinsen zu einem Kichern und den ganzen Weg nach Haus lachte der Fuchs aus vollem Hals.

"King of the Forest," said Fox to himself with a smile. His smile grew into a grin, and his grin grew into a giggle, and Fox laughed out loud all the way home.

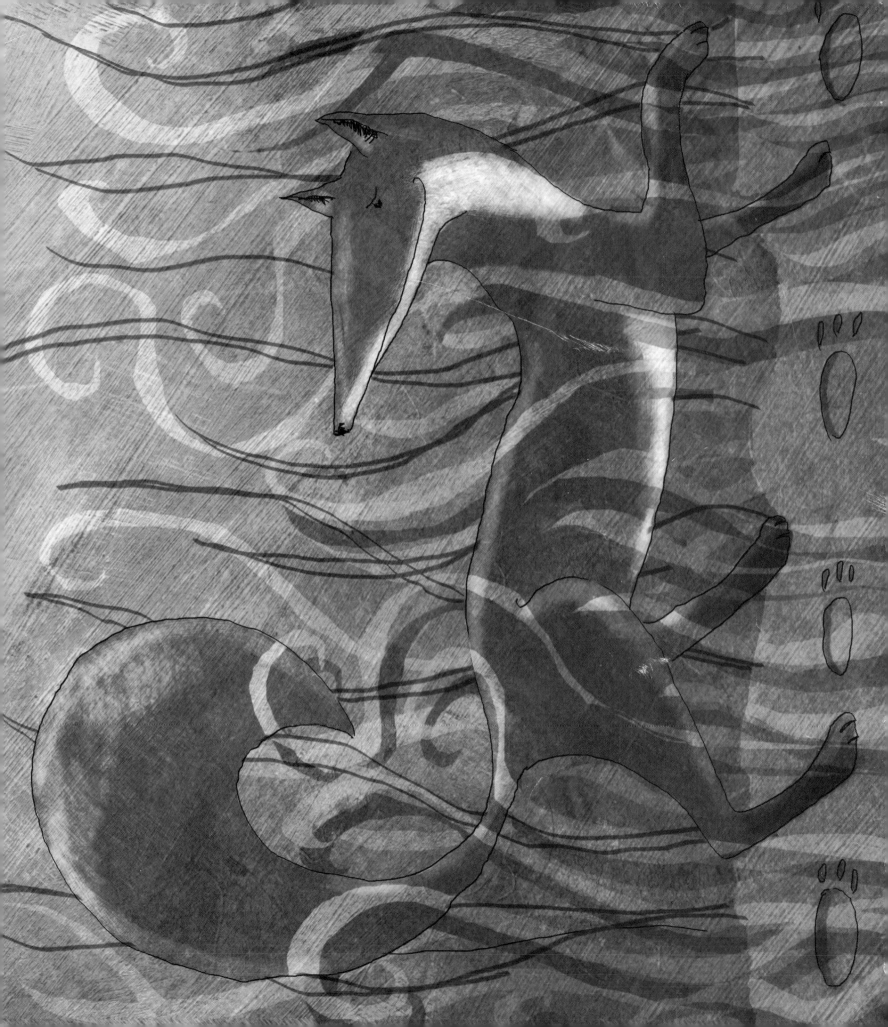

To my Nana, with love ~ DC

For my wife, Alex ~ J

First published in 2006 by Mantra Lingua Ltd
Global House, 303 Ballards Lane
London N12 8NP
www.mantralingua.com